TEMPLE RUN

RUN FOR YOUR LIFE!

™

ARCTIC
RESCUE

EGMONT

With special thanks to Adrian Bott.

EGMONT

We bring stories to life

First published in Great Britain 2014 by Egmont UK Limited
The Yellow Building, 1 Nicholas Road, London W11 4AN

Cover illustration by Jacopo Camagni
Inside illustrations by Artful Doodlers
Text & illustrations copyright © 2014 Imangi Studios, LLC

ISBN 978 1 4052 7501 9

www.ImangiStudios.com
www.Egmont.co.uk

57743/1

A CIP catalogue record for this title is available from the British Library.
Printed and bound in Great Britain by the CPI Group.

FSC
MIX
Paper
FSC® C018306

EGMONT LUCKY COIN

Our story began over a century ago, when seventeen-year-old
Egmont Harald Petersen found a coin in the street.

He was on his way to buy a flyswatter, a small hand-operated
printing machine that he then set up in his tiny apartment.

The coin brought him such good luck that today Egmont has
offices in over 30 countries around the world. And that lucky
coin is still kept at the company's head offices in Denmark.

'We're here,' says Officer Barry Bones, as your little plane touches down on the airstrip.

You look out the window at the white, cold landscape of the Arctic wilderness. It's not snowing right now, but by the look of this place, it will be soon.

You're in the far north, almost at the limit of civilisation. Past this point, you don't expect to see many people. Moose, maybe, and beavers. Perhaps wolves too.

Scarlett Fox pulls her red hair into a loose ponytail and checks her laptop. 'No new messages from Guy. How about you, kid?'

'No,' you tell her. It's the truth . . . this time.

*

Guy Dangerous is missing.

He's gone missing before, of course. The world-famous explorer has a knack for getting himself in trouble. You've got a dozen news stories bookmarked in your browser back home:

DANGEROUS VANISHES IN JUNGLE!
EXPLORER MISSING IN DESERT!
DANGEROUS EVAPORATES AT SEA!

You're the founder of the Guy Dangerous Young Explorers Club. These stories are the sort of thing you keep track of. If there were ever a Guy Dangerous trivia quiz, you'd ace it.

But this time, Guy's been gone for too long. You may have been just a fan at first, but you and Guy have been emailing for a while now, and you think of him as a friend.

The trouble all began a few weeks ago, when Guy announced he was going on a trek into the far north to test his survival instincts. Right from the start you've known there was more to it than that, because he contacted you – and only you – personally.

'*I'm on the trail of something big,*' read his email message. '*Something that could put me in danger. If other people find out what I'm looking for, they'll stop at nothing to get there first.*'

You read the message again and again. It didn't make any sense. What could possibly be of interest out there in the frozen wilderness? Had Guy found some sort of ancient ruin, or a shipwreck maybe? Perhaps the remains of an Arctic expedition? But then, why would that mean Guy was in danger?

Not long after, Guy sent you another email – but this one was scrambled and incomplete:

'*Need . . . help. Come looking for me . . . track down . . . Bones . . . his badge . . . trust him.*'

At first, you thought it was bizarre. Bones? A skeleton with a badge? But you did some research and found out Guy had a friend called Barry Bones, who was a police officer. That explained what the 'badge' must be.

So you contacted Barry Bones, who promptly offered to help you go and rescue Guy. You didn't think your parents would be cool with it, but Barry managed to persuade them. He is a policeman, after all – and besides, it would be good publicity for the Young Explorers Club.

You grinned as you looked through the plans Barry drew up. This is a rescue mission, but Barry had made it seem like an adventure, too. He'd arranged for the two of you to take a dog sled across the snow. For the first time in your life, you'd be following in Guy Dangerous's footsteps – literally!

But as you were getting ready to set out, another old friend of Guy's arrived – this time, uninvited.

'Sorry to barge in,' said Scarlett Fox, 'but I found out about this expedition of yours, and I wanted to help. Guy's an old friend. We've been in dozens of scrapes together. If anyone can find him, I can!'

You and Barry had little choice but to bring Scarlett along. You're not sure if you can trust her yet, so you decide to keep Guy's messages to yourself.

★

At the little Arctic airport, Barry pulls out his files. 'Two weeks ago, Guy said he was camping in a pine forest called Kalinki Ridge,' he tells you. 'It's not far from here. Might be a good place to start the search.'

'Anyone but Guy would have used a GPS, and we'd be able to go straight to him,' Scarlett sighs, shaking her head. 'But he's a stubborn old coot, isn't he?' She winks at you.

You know what she means. Unlike Scarlett, Guy doesn't use gadgets. He considers it 'cheating'. Guy prefers to pit his wits against Nature. You just have to hope that Nature didn't win this round.

The forest's name is the only solid information you've got on his whereabouts. The challenge is to figure out where he might have gone next. You all head into the airport cafe for a mug of cocoa and a hot meal. Your breath steams in the clean, icy air.

Barry shows you his planned route on a map. 'Reshranka is the nearest town to Kalinki Ridge. Guy might have gone through there on his way north. Let's try to pick up his trail there.'

You look at the huge section of open tundra between here and the little town. 'We can still take the dog sled, right?'

'Of course!' Barry grins. 'I've made all the arrangements. The huskies are waiting for us.'

'Awesome!' Huskies are great dogs – and travelling overland will let you look for other clues, too.

But the look Scarlett gives Barry is colder than the frost on the windows. 'You must be joking. I'm not riding overland with a pack of hounds! Besides, Guy won't have gone to Reshranka.'

'And what makes you so sure?' Barry demands.

'Guy wouldn't have gone to a *town*. He'd see that as too convenient! You know what he's like – the great explorer, man against the wild, all that malarkey. No, we need to fly further north. A *lot* further.'

Scarlett explains that she wants to fly to the tiny village of Tompakotac, which is many miles further north on the edge of the mountains. The dog sled idea is out. To reach Tompakotac, you'll have to take

a small private plane.

Barry folds his arms. 'I ain't flying out on some crazy trip to the middle of nowhere!'

'Fine. You go and have your little sledding holiday. In the meantime, Guy's *real* friends can go and help him!' Scarlett gives you a meaningful look.

It seems Barry and Scarlett refuse to agree to each other's plans. Each one is determined to do it their way. You'll have to choose who to go with.

To go with Barry on the dog sled, turn to page 9.

To fly with Scarlett, go to page 59.

You try to fight off the demon monkeys, but there are just too many of them and you're overwhelmed.

They leave you buried in a snow bank for a while until you're frozen solid. Then they take you out and start licking your head, making happy noises. Congratulations, you've been turned into an explorer popsicle! Did you know you have a fruity tang that demon monkeys go crazy for?

RUN AGAIN? TURN TO PAGE **5**

Scarlett rolls her eyes and gets up to leave. 'Fine. Whatever. I'll fly up to Tompakotac and rescue Guy by myself.'

'Have fun!' Barry grins. 'Don't forget to write!'

You take a taxi out to the lodge where the sled is being prepared for you. You can't help staring out the window at how strange everything looks here. The land is bare except for trees waving in the wind. The hills are covered with snow. It's bleak, but it's breathtaking too, like being on another planet.

At the lodge, you meet a grey-haired woman called Mary who reminds you of someone's crazy aunt. 'Come round and meet the dogs!' she says.

The Siberian Huskies are milling about in their enclosure. Six pairs of ice-blue eyes look up at you. You offer the largest dog your hand to sniff and in seconds they're barking and howling and jumping all over you excitedly. Mary tells you their names: Dandy, Jester, Maestro, Kirk, Brucie and Captain Jack. 'Look after them, and they'll look after you,' she says, as they leap and bark.

The sled itself is quite small, with a single flat seat for the passenger, lined with reindeer skins. The driver steers from the back of the sled, using their feet to brake. Barry explains that you'll take it in turns to drive, and he's going to go first.

Mary prepares you for your dog-sledding expedition across the snowy tundra. She briefs you on the important safety points, number one of which is to never, *ever* let go of the sled. 'They're good dogs, but don't fool yerself – they *will* take off without you, and they'll pull the sled with 'em,' she says. 'And it's a long walk home!'

Once your tents, ice axes, food and water are all packed, you settle in for a good night's sleep. You snuggle down under the sealskin blanket, making the most of the warmth. From here on in, it's going to get a lot colder!

★

Morning dawns. Mary makes you a huge breakfast and waves you goodbye. You get comfortable in the sled while Barry steps on behind, ready to drive.

It's a clear, bright day and the world looks newly made, pure-white snow gleaming in the early sun.

Barry urges the dogs on the way dog-sledders have done for years: 'Hike! Hike!'

You're flung back in your seat. The dog sled rockets over the smooth snow like a runaway go-cart. The huskies bound along as if they're having their first exercise in weeks. You grip the sled tightly, remembering what Mary said about never letting go. You may be a passenger, but this is NOT a restful way to travel. In fact, it's terrifying! Those dogs are made of pure muscle.

Soon, the lodge is just a distant shape on the horizon behind you. The open hills are rushing past. Cold air makes your nose tingle. You see a body of water off to the left, glittering in the morning sun, with huge ice floes drifting over it. Are those dark shapes on the ice seals, you wonder?

It doesn't take you long to calm down and start enjoying the ride. This really is an amazing way of going places. But just as you're getting into it, Barry calls out, 'Whoa!' The huskies slow down and stop.

'What's wrong?' you ask.

'Nothing's wrong. It's your turn to drive!'

You gulp. So soon? Well, you'd better get on with it. Barry makes sure you're secure in the driving position, gripping the handlebar, before he sits down. You run through the commands in your mind. *Haw* to turn left, *gee* to turn right . . . And to brake, you slam your feet down on two rickety levers.

'Hike!' you yell. 'Hike! Hike!'

You aren't prepared for the sheer force of a group of dogs all pulling at once. It's frightening at first, but soon becomes the biggest thrill of your life. You pass another team and give them a friendly nod, your hands still gripping the bar tightly in front of you. This isn't going so badly!

Barry twists around to get your attention. 'Where do you want to head to, bud?'

'What are the options?' you ask.

'Well, we can take the main route to Reshranka,

like everyone else does,' Barry says. 'There's plenty of people around, it'll be fast and safe, and Guy probably went through Reshranka too. We can talk to the folks there, ask if they've seen him and if he said anything more about his plans.'

'OK, what's the other option?'

'It's risky,' Barry says, sounding a bit cagey.

You laugh. 'I don't mind.'

'OK then! Option two is we head straight for Kalinki Ridge, the forest where Guy said he was camping out. We can look for clues there. He might even have left a message for us.'

You mull it over, holding on tight as the dogs whisk you over the snow.

Do you want to take the quicker, safer route to Reshranka? Go to page 15.

Or would you rather risk the wilderness and head to Kalinki Ridge instead? Go to page 18.

14

Scarlett races off up the cliff as if her life depended on it – which it does.

Unfortunately speed makes her careless and she slips and falls. She dangles from the rope, her weight threatening to tear you off the cliff too.

'Save me!' she begs.

You're not sure the spike you just knocked in will take your weight.

Do you try to pull Scarlett back up with both hands, even though it might mean you both fall? Or do you use only one hand to pull her up, hanging on to the cliff with the other hand for safety?

To try using both hands to haul Scarlett up, turn to page 109.

To hang on to the cliff and just use one hand, turn to page 86.

'Let's take the safe route for now,' you say to Barry. 'There's going to be plenty of risks to go round later on, right?'

'I'm sure there will,' Barry agrees. 'You got a good head on your shoulders, kid. I can see why Guy respects you.'

Then, in the distance, a wolf howls. The sound makes you shiver. Just as well you didn't head to Kalinki Ridge, you think to yourself. There's danger out here as well as beauty.

With only a short break for lunch – which is beef tea, protein bars and crackers – you make good time. There are black clouds on the far horizon.

You wonder how Scarlett is getting on. Has she flown into a storm?

You arrive in Reshranka at sunset. It's a small town, but everyone seems friendly. Barry tethers the dogs and you go to find something to eat.

The local diner is made of logs and has antlers on the wall. Inside, next to a roaring fire, you get talking to an old man who remembers when Guy came through here. Barry excitedly takes notes.

'Nice young fella, he was. Good manners. Had kind of wild eyes. Thought he was on to something important.'

'Did he say what it was?' Barry asks.

'Nope. "It'll change the world of archaeology," was all he said.'

'Do you know which way he went from here?' you ask. This is great. You finally have a lead!

The old geezer scratches his chin. 'If I was you, I'd keep going north to Tompakotac. Your man was going to go by way of Wendigo Plateau, but I'd steer clear of that place.'

The diner has gone quiet. 'Why?' you ask. You notice people are staring at you.

The old guy just shrugs, but won't tell you why – no matter how much you pester him.

Barry gets up. 'Reckon we've got all we can out of this place. Let's go.'

On your way out of the diner, a little kid stops you. 'Don't go to Wendigo Plateau,' he whispers. 'There are howling spirits there. Ghosts in the snow.'

You hurry away. Barry insists that you go to Wendigo Plateau as soon as possible. If it's risky, Guy Dangerous won't have been able to resist it.

Do you strike out now, even though it's dark and the weather is growing worse? Go to page 22.

Or do you wait until morning before setting out, and hope Guy isn't in too much peril? Head to page 26.

The sled races on through the Arctic wilderness. Soon there's no sign of human life at all. You and Barry are the only people for miles around. You wonder how you're ever going to find Guy in all of this snowy emptiness. You check your phone, just in case he's sent you a new message, but of course you're a long way from the nearest radio tower.

'There's Kalinki Ridge up ahead!' Barry tells you. It's a dark mass of trees on the side of a rocky rise. Even from this distance, it looks creepy somehow.

Barry urges the dogs on. You're travelling past the shores of a sky-blue lake that shines bright as a mirror. What would it be like to crack the ice and jump into that water? You reckon you'd freeze to a solid lump in less than a minute.

You draw nearer and nearer to Kalinki Ridge. One moment the huskies are running happily, the

next they go crazy, barking and tugging. Barry hollers at them to stop. You see something jutting up out of the snow.

'That's a broken moose antler,' Barry says. He's using his Cop Voice, you notice. When Barry's being super-serious, his voice changes. 'And see how the snow's all churned up? No wonder the dogs are freaking out. There's been some kind of a fight here. I just hope Guy wasn't mixed up in it.'

But knowing Guy, you think, *he might have been.*

Tracks lead off away from the fight scene. Do you follow them to see what – or who – made them? Go to page 28.

Or, to ignore the tracks and keep going towards Kalinki Ridge, head to page 33.

Barry and Doctor Finnegan try to stop you, but it's too late. You bang on the doors, on the walls, on anything you can lay your hands on. Eventually, you hear the trapper trudging over to the hut.

'Excuse me, sir?' you yell through the tiny window. 'Can we maybe pay you to let us out of here?'

The trapper comes and peers in at you. 'How much you got?'

You rummage in your pockets, but only come up with a few coins. Barry has a bag of dog biscuits, and Doctor Finnegan a near-empty bottle of cough syrup. The trapper snorts. 'Nice try, kid.'

He turns to leave. Your temper snaps. 'Just let us out of here, you smelly jerk!'

The trapper pauses. 'Now why in heck would I want to do that?'

'Because people are going to come looking for us. You won't get away with this.'

The guy rubs his hairy chin. 'You got a point, kid. People will come looking for you. I better make sure you don't ever get found. I know just the place . . .'

(Let's just fast-forward through the next bit, if that's OK with you. This bad guy is very good at staying undiscovered. He doesn't want to talk. All three of you go missing.)

Fortunately, you're discovered six thousand years later, frozen solid in a glacier. You're so well preserved that the surgeons of the future are able to put your brain into a robot body, which is actually kind of awesome!

But unfortunately, your programming can't access files older than four thousand years, so you never do find out whether Guy was ever rescued.

RUN AGAIN? TURN TO PAGE **5**

Heading into the snowy wilderness after dark wasn't a brilliant idea. The weather gets worse and soon swirling flakes are all you can see.

You press on regardless.

The problem with wandering about in a blizzard after dark is that it's hard to tell the difference between an ordinary firm snow layer and the covering over a crevasse. You go tumbling down into a deep, dark hole.

The good news is that Barry is able to save the dogs. Huskies are cute, aren't they? But it's the end of the line for you!

RUN AGAIN? TURN TO PAGE 5

You sprint away from the plateau, still feeling shaken up from your tumble.

The trapper is faster. Through the mounds of ice and snow, you catch glimpses of him running after you like a maddened bear.

It looks like you'll never make it. As if things couldn't get any worse, you slip and twist your ankle. You crawl into a small cave in the ice to hide.

Then you see a little huddle of Arctic fox cubs hiding there with you. You peer at them, amazed. Their little button noses are so cute you just want to *boop* them. You wonder where their mother and father are. You hope the trappers didn't get them.

You hear the trapper hollering. 'Where did that kid go? Find 'em, *now!*'

Suddenly you realise it's your destiny to help the little cubs. A glimmer of a plan appears in your mind. It's crazy, but you've got to try.

With renewed courage, you grit your teeth and limp out to confront the trapper. 'Here I am,' you yell, hoping like mad that Barry is somewhere nearby.

The trapper thinks you're giving up. 'Sensible kid,' he gloats, as he stalks over. 'Reckon I'll send your parents a ransom demand. I was planning on retiring soon anyway.'

'Not so fast,' you tell him coolly, holding your ground. 'I'd turn around, if I were you.'

'You think I'm falling for that?'

You shrug. 'Whatever.'

That's when Barry lunges from behind a mound of ice and snaps a pair of handcuffs on him. 'Get on your knees, creep! You're under arrest.'

The other trapper runs like crazy. Barry contacts the police at Reshranka, and they tell you to sit tight and wait for help to arrive.

With your ankle twisted, you won't be able to help Guy out like you hoped. That's too bad. There's nothing to do but sit here and wait.

But as you sit, one of the cubs comes lolloping out and curls up next to you. Then another comes and climbs into your lap. Then another, and another. Barry just stares as the Arctic fox cubs pile on you in a furry heap. 'How did you do that?' he whispers.

'Maybe they think I'm their mum or dad?' you say, as a cub licks your face.

'Could be,' Barry says, shaking his head. 'Bud, I'd say you've got a new family to look after.'

These little guys should probably be in a zoo, but you wonder if your parents will let you keep them anyway. Maybe you could build an Arctic fox run in your bedroom . . .

RUN AGAIN? TURN TO PAGE 5

You spend a comfortable night in Reshranka. No messages come through from Guy. 'Hang in there, buddy,' you whisper to your phone. 'We're coming to find you.'

Morning dawns. The day is overcast and a chill wind is blowing — a bad omen — and the dogs are skittish and uneasy. You say your goodbyes and head out for the plateau.

Before long, Wendigo Plateau comes in view. You can make out a raised section of land with what looks like a group of huts on it. A hunter's cabin, perhaps, or an ice fisher's lodge?

As you get closer, a long, baleful howl resounds across the tundra. The huskies howl too. It seems like the noise has spooked them.

Barry gives you a look. 'Are you thinking what I'm thinking?'

Your mind goes back to that kid at Reshranka. What was it he said? Ghosts in the snow . . .

Then you notice strange, luminous shapes darting about among the huts. This is so creepy!

Your gut tells you that something's not right about this place. But there's every chance that Guy is somewhere nearby – or, hero that he is, tried to investigate and got into trouble.

Do you want to check out the group of huts?
Turn to page 42.

Or would you prefer to leave well alone, and keep heading north? Turn to page 68.

You follow the tracks across the snow, holding the handlebar tight. Barry points out the different animal prints. 'You got hooves and a lot of paws, see? Looks like whatever was hurt was brought down by a pack of wolves.'

The trail ends near the foot of Kalinki Ridge, behind a snowdrift that hides what's going on until you're right up close. It's not Guy, you're relieved to see. It's just a dead moose. You can tell it's freshly killed, because the Arctic wolves who brought it down are still setting upon it. Feeding time! There must be five or six of them. The huskies yelp and whine, eager to get out of here.

'We're going to be OK,' Barry reassures you. 'Wolves hardly ever attack people.'

The wolves look up from their meal and snarl at you. 'I don't think these wolves got the memo,' you tell him.

'They don't look friendly, do they?' Barry gulps. 'Something must have driven them crazy. Maybe they're starving, or there's something in the water.'

You don't have time to talk about it, because next thing you know, the wolves are charging at you! You have to act fast to protect the dogs, the sled, and yourself. Pick a direction to steer the sled in, and hurry!

Do you try to turn around and head back overland? Dash to page 36.

Or do you take a huge risk and cut across the frozen lake? It might bear your weight, but it also might not. Race to page 39.

Barry hammers on the door of the biggest hut. A surly, hairy man comes to answer it. He stinks like a dead bear. 'Yeah?'

Barry flashes his badge. 'Police. I need to talk to you about this little fur-trapping operation of yours.'

The man snorts and spits. 'What about it? It's all above board.'

'I need to see your licence,' Barry says.

'Anything you say, officer,' sneers the trapper. 'Walk this way and I'll show you my papers.'

'If you're such a good guy,' you ask him, as you trudge through the snow, 'then why do you use those gizmos to make ghost noises and creepy lights?'

'Because it keeps busybodies out of my business!' the trapper snaps at you. 'Or it used to, anyway.'

'Just show us your licence, sir, and we'll be on our way,' says Barry, using his Cop Voice again. He gives you a warning look that says, *this guy is trouble*.

The trapper shows you to a small hut with an open door. 'In you go. That's where I keep my paperwork.'

You step forwards. 'Isn't it a bit dark in here?'

Barry follows you. 'Not much of an office. Are you sure –?'

Before Barry can say another word, the trapper shoves you both inside and slams the door! You hear him slide a bolt home ...

Head to page 45 to see what happens next!

The paw prints lead up and up, past the Research Institute and on into the mountains. You follow them. Your path takes you up scree slopes where you have to grapple for handholds, along narrow ridges where you have to press your whole body to the ice face to pass, and up sheer surfaces where you need your ice axe to climb at all.

Whatever these creatures are, they're *very* good climbers. You struggle to follow their trail and wonder if they came down from the very highest peak of the mountain. Surely there can't be much more of this?

As you're thinking about turning back, you see a gaping cave mouth way above you. It's on an ice shelf that sticks out like a balcony. That must be where the creatures came from! You haul yourself up.

It's an exhausting hike, but you make it. As you draw nearer, you realise it's no ordinary cave. It's some kind of ice temple!

Head to page 140.

You steer the sled in among the looming pines of Kalinki Ridge. You know Guy was here, less than two weeks ago. You think back to all the articles you've read on the Young Explorers Club wiki. You'll need to draw on that knowledge if you're going to save Guy's life.

'So if I was Guy,' Barry asks you, 'where would I make my camp?'

You know the answer instantly. 'Somewhere out of the wind and easy to defend.'

You and Barry start searching, looking for places where Guy might have pitched his tent. It doesn't take long before you spot a torn piece of green tent fabric among some bracken. Then you find the remains of a campfire and some scraps of clothing.

'This could be it,' you tell Barry, your heart pounding. *If this is Guy's stuff, why is it flung everywhere?*

'Someone camped here, all right,' Barry says. 'But it wasn't Guy. Look at this.' He holds up a notebook. 'Doctor Marie Finnegan. I wonder who she is?'

'Or was,' you say with a shudder.

34

You and Barry search through Doctor Finnegan's scattered things and try to piece the story together.

'She was heading to a group of huts on Wendigo Plateau, investigating something illegal,' Barry says, reading the notebook. 'It says she heard strange, ghostly howling coming from there. I guess she ran into trouble, because she hasn't been back for days.'

You spot something shiny near the dead campfire. A pocketknife, with the initials 'GD' carved into the handle. 'This belongs to Guy!' you yell, snatching it up. 'That means they must have met.'

'She was probably the last person to see Guy before he vanished!' Barry says. 'That's our best lead so far.'

It's decision time.

If you head for Wendigo Plateau, you can try to find Doctor Finnegan and see if she knows where Guy went. Go to page 42.

If you'd rather keep heading north towards Tompakotac and look for signs of Guy along the way, turn to page 68.

You and Barry sneak around the group of fur trappers' huts. The only sound is your breathing and the crunch of your footsteps on the snow.

There's a nasty-looking guy on the corner pacing back and forth. You wonder if he's just out here for the fresh air, but then you see he's got binoculars slung around his neck. He's got to be a lookout. And people like *you* are just who he's looking out for.

You're sneaking up behind him, so he hasn't seen you yet, but he could turn around at any moment. You can smell him from here. He stinks of unwashed clothes and bad sardines. Barry holds his nose.

You need to get past this guy somehow. How are you going to avoid him?

Do you duck into a small old-looking hut?
Go to page 48.

Or climb up a ladder to the roof and sneak over his head? Go to page 50.

In all the confusion of the wolf attack, you accidentally let go of the sled. This is the one thing you must *never, ever* do. The huskies race off to the right and you suddenly go flying into the snow.

You pull yourself to your feet as the huskies race away. The sled disappears off into the distance, with Barry yelling and waving his arms, unable to control the dogs from his passenger's seat. Next second, the wolves pounce.

To your amazement, the wolves take you in. They raise you as one of their own, bringing you food and teaching you their wild ways. In time, you become head of the pack. They give you the honourable name of Runs-On-Two-Legs, pronounced *grawrooogr* in wolf. In time, you return to human civilisation, where you use your wolfen skills to fight crime in the city.

Only joking! They eat you.

RUN AGAIN? TURN TO PAGE **5**

You skid down the ice chute, moving faster and faster, until you're sure you won't be able to stop. Luckily, the channel levels out. You go rocketing out of the end like a cork from a bottle, spin around a few times and come to a complete stop.

Once the dizziness has passed, you get to your feet and shine the light around. You're in some sort of ice gallery. It's a cavern with smooth blue-white walls. Carved into the walls are ice sculptures of people wearing strange clothing, like tribal wear from hundreds of years ago. You take a better look. The detail on the sculptures is crazily good. In fact, you get the feeling these are real people who've been turned to solid ice. How freaky is THAT?

Then you see it – a golden idol, half-frozen in the far wall. There, next to it, is Guy Dangerous! He's partly frozen in the ice, but he's still alive. You don't know *how*, but you're too relieved to care.

You see he's holding his phone in one hand. The other one's frozen in the ice. He must have been sending messages one-handed while barely conscious. So that's why his messages have been so short and garbled and hard to understand!

'Guy!' you shout. 'Hang in there! I'll get you out!'

Guy groans. You'll have to be quick.

You start running towards him, but then you remember Guy's rule for young explorers: always think things through! You stop and think it over.

Guy should have frozen to death by now, but somehow he's still alive. He flicks his eyes at you, almost like he's trying to say something . . . but what?

You're not sure how much longer Guy has left. You pull out your ice axe, thinking you can hack at the ice until he can break free. Then you pause. There's something weird going on here, and the idol has to be the key to it. Maybe you should focus on the idol?

To use your ice axe to free Guy first, head to page 133.

To cut the idol out of the ice first, go to page 149.

You yell to the huskies, hoping they'll obey you. Luckily, you must have what it takes to lead a team of sled dogs, because they rush out across the ice without hesitating. The wolves are close behind you, snapping and snarling at your heels. 'Come on!' you urge the dogs. 'Good dogs. Keep it up!'

The ice below you groans. You hope it's strong enough to bear your weight.

Behind you, the wolves skid and slide on the ice. With a sound like cracking timber, part of the ice breaks and a wolf is left floundering in freezing water. As he heaves his bedraggled body back out again, the rest of the pack give up chasing you. Obviously they'd rather feast on moose than hunt you and your dogs down.

You bring the sled back across the ice towards the lake's shore. The ice creaks ominously beneath you, but it doesn't give. There's a bump as you head up the lakeside, and then the sled is rushing across the snow-covered earth once again.

You're glad to be back on firm ground.

'Good work,' Barry says. 'That could have been nasty.'

'Now what?' you ask him.

Barry glances up at the darkening sky. 'We get out of here. We've seen no sign from Guy, so let's press on northwards. We should reach Tompakotac in a few days. Scarlett's already there, of course.'

'Shouldn't we have heard from her by now?'

'I was afraid you'd say that,' sighs Barry. 'I guess we've got two explorers to rescue . . .'

You forge on ahead into the wilderness.

Head to page 68.

It's not a good survival technique to push yourself beyond your limit, especially in freezing conditions. You trudge on until you fall over by the wayside, utterly tired out.

By morning you're a solid frozen lump, covered in frost. But you'd make a fantastic Christmas decoration! All sparkly and magical . . .

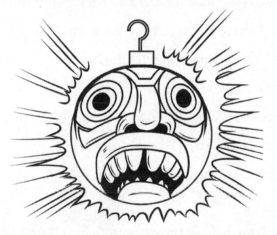

RUN AGAIN? TURN TO PAGE **5**

You approach the huts on Wendigo Plateau. The howling is driving the huskies crazy, so you tether them safely before moving on.

You peer through some binoculars and notice a funny-looking machine among the huts, like a speaker with a dance floor light projector fixed to it. The closer you get, the more obvious it becomes that the machine is making both the howling noise and the strange lights. There's nothing ghostly about it at all. You point it out to Barry.

'The old fake spook routine, huh?' He grins. 'Now, doesn't that explain a whole lot? Someone's up to no good here.'

'What do you think it is?' you ask.

'At a guess, it's fur trappers.'

You frown. 'Isn't fur trapping allowed up here?'

'It is allowed, so long as you don't use cruel traps or hunt any endangered animals,' Barry says. 'But this operation looks illegal as heck – why else would they try to hide what they're up to? Just the sort of thing Guy Dangerous would have tried to bust.'

'On his own,' you add.

'Without backup. Armed with just his fists.'

'Yup,' you say. 'That's Guy all right.'

You and Barry agree you need to get inside those huts. The only question is how. Barry suggests the full-on cop approach – namely, banging on the door, flashing his badge and demanding to look around. But you think Guy would probably have sneaked in, and as founder of the Guy Dangerous Young Explorers Club, you ought to know.

To try Barry's method, go to page 30.

To sneak in like you think Guy would have, go to page 35.

The canteen is completely abandoned. There are unfinished meals on the plates. Looks like the scientists ran away in a hurry. There's no sign of whatever scared them.

You check the kitchen and find a big selection of ready meals in the freezer. Who knew scientists liked mac'n'cheese so much? Maybe it boosts your brain or something. You're starving hungry, so you help yourself to a meal before heading back out.

As you leave, you notice some coarse white hairs caught around the door. You wonder if a polar bear attacked the base. But a polar bear would have left different tracks. They run on four paws. Whatever left the prints behind here was running on two feet. Was this place overrun by a Yeti? Or something worse?

Time to move on. Which pod do you want to check out next?

You can investigate the lab on page 135.

Or you can take a look at the dormitory on page 105.

Great, you think. You were meant to be finding Guy, but now you and Barry have been taken prisoner and locked in a stupid little hut!

'Nice to have company,' says a pale woman with glasses and short hair. She's sitting in the shadows. She coughs, and then gives you a weak grin. 'I'm Doctor Finnegan. Who the heck are you?'

While Barry explains, you try the hut door. It's securely bolted. You're not getting out the way you came in, that's for sure.

Over the next five minutes, Doctor Finnegan – who keeps coughing and shivering – tells you about how she's been looking into the illegal fur trapping. She tried to explore the huts, but got caught. 'I guess I should stick to medicine and leave the adventures for people like Guy Dangerous,' she sighs.

'So you met Guy?' you ask, excited.

She nods and coughs again. 'He's good people. Gave me his pocketknife when I lost my own. I did ask him to help me take these bad guys down, but he couldn't stick around. He was heading north.'

'Did he tell you where?' Barry says, whipping out his notebook again. It's amazing how Barry can just drop into Cop Mode and out again, like a transforming robot.

'Yeah. He told me – *cough* – he was making for the Aurora Research Institute near Tompakotac. I guess you won't have heard of that place. It's pretty secret. With good reason.'

This mystery is deepening by the minute. You wonder what the Aurora Research Institute might be. Then, in a jolt, it hits you. *Did Scarlett know about Aurora? Is that why she wanted to go to Tompakotac?*

Doctor Finnegan gets to her feet, steadying herself against the wall. 'So. Who's up for busting out?'

You and Barry think that sounds like a great idea. The only thing is: how are you going to do it?

Do you yell for the trapper and try to bribe him into letting you go? Go to page 20.

Or do you try a crazy Guy Dangerous-style escape attempt? Go to page 51.

You sprint like crazy and then, just to be extra-careful, you burrow down into the snow for a while. When you feel it's safe, you head back to the tent, only to see that the bear has helped itself to your food. There's no sign of the bear, though, so at least it doesn't want to eat *you*.

It's the middle of the night, you're starving hungry, and you're miles from anywhere. This is a survival situation. What would Guy Dangerous do?

You could try to make a hole in the frozen lake and fish through it. Or you could set off and try to make it to the town of Tompakotac, which is still pretty far away — though they'll probably have food there.

To try fishing, go to page 126.

To head towards Tompakotac, run to page 49.

The hut seems like a good place to hide, at least at first. But then the trapper sees your two pairs of footprints in the snow, leading right to the door.

The last thing you see before you black out is his grinning face.

Wake up on page 45.

After trudging through snow and ice for an age, you see buildings in the far distance. They're only simple wooden houses, but there are lots of them. Tompakotac! Civilisation at last!

The thought of reaching safety gives you fresh energy, and you stride onwards. The sky grows lighter and you can make out more detail.

That's weird. Tompakotac seems strangely still and silent. You can't see any smoke from fires, nor hear even the slightest sound. You shrug and carry on. Then, some way off the path, you notice something bizarre – a house made from ice, halfway up a mountain slope! Oddly coloured lights flicker from within. You shake yourself, but you're not dreaming.

Do you want to visit the strange, glowing ice-house? Where there's light, there could be people to help you. Head to page 89.

Or do you keep on for Tompakotac? Head to page 122.

You clamber up on to the prefab hut. Barry climbs up behind you, huffing. The guard scratches his backside. He hasn't noticed a thing.

From up here you can see the whole area. There are all kinds of pelts hanging up here. Arctic wolf pelts, sealskins, beaver . . . Whatever this guy is up to, it's not legal. You take some pictures on your phone. Evidence! You're patting yourself on the back for being so clever when Barry, behind you, puts his foot through the roof. *CRASH!*

'Who's there?' yells the guard. He runs around and stares up at you. 'Hey! We got snoopers!'

Barry tries to pull his leg back out of the hole in the roof, but he just ends up making more noise. You're going to have to deal with this situation alone.

What are you going to do?

To leap down from the roof and run for your life, head to page 23.

Or if that seems too risky, you could surrender. Head to page 45.

'We need to break out of here,' you tell Barry and Doctor Finnegan. 'Think. What would Guy Dangerous do?'

'You should get that on a T-shirt,' the doctor sniffs. 'WWGDD?'

Barry shrugs. 'You're the expert, bud. You know more about Guy Dangerous than either of us. So you tell us what he'd do.'

You think back through all the wild and crazy Guy stories you've ever heard. You're sure there was one where he was stuck in a jam like this . . .

Yes! Now you remember! There's a story from Guy's website about how he was once locked in a portable toilet. He escaped by rocking back and forth until it overturned and slid down a slope. He came out smelling disgusting, but alive.

Maybe that could work here. This hut used to be a container of some kind. It's not fixed to the ground. You explain your plan to the others.

Lucky for you, the spooky sound machine is still running. The sound of the pre-recorded howling hides the noise as the three of you rock the hut back and forth.

'Keep it up!' Barry roars. 'Nearly there . . .'

With a crash, the hut overturns. It goes tumbling down the side of the plateau. The three of you are thrown about inside like passengers on a funfair ride, only without safety belts.

Eventually it stops. The hut, door and all, is smashed to bits. You're battered and bruised, but you can escape!

Up above, the trapper is yelling in fury. He's coming after you, and he has a friend with him!

The dog sled is tethered nearby, but to reach it you'll have to run *towards* the bad guys. If you reach it in time, though, it'll get you out of here fast.

To run for the sled, head to page 56.

Or if you think it's safer for the three of you to split up and flee the bad guys on foot, run to page 23.

'I'll come back to Reshranka with the two of you,' you say. 'Safety in numbers, right?'

Barry glances up to the sky, where a few white flakes are starting to fall. 'Good call. We've got snow coming. Lots of it.'

You race off back towards Reshranka with Doctor Finnegan and Barry in the sled. It's level ground here, so the dogs can go flat out and you hardly need to do any braking at all.

Reshranka comes into view in the distance – and that's when you hear the growl of a snowmobile. It's one of the fur trappers, and he's chasing you down!

'Hang on!' you yell to Barry and Doctor Finnegan. She looks terrified. Barry just nods grimly. You wish he was steering the sled and not you.

The snowmobile comes closer and closer. It looks like he's going to try to ram you! Barry points out a group of pine trees over to one side. 'Get in among those trees if you can!'

You shout to the tired dogs. They zoom off

towards the trees. Barry grabs the doctor, who almost tips out of the sled. The snowmobile keeps coming.

You cross your fingers. You're going to have to try something crazy. With the fur trapper only yards away, you steer the dogs to head left and then right. You swerve around the trees like you're in a dodgem car. Barry and the doctor are flung off and land, gasping, in the snow.

The trapper tries to follow, but he's going too fast. The snowmobile goes berserk and flings him into a tree. *Oof.* Trees hurt!

You bring the sled to a welcome stop, breathing hard, feeling like you got away by the skin of your teeth.

Once the bad guy comes round – with a splitting headache – Barry puts him under arrest. He makes a call to the police in Reshranka, who are soon on the way.

'We're going to have to put the search for Guy Dangerous on ice for a while,' Barry says with a sigh.

'He'd want us to bust these bad guys,' you say. 'And I think he'd be proud.'

You know you've done the right thing here, but you can't help wondering what Guy is up to, wherever he is. What was the secret he claimed to have found, and just how much did Scarlett know about it? Whatever happened to her, anyway? Simply mystifying!

RUN AGAIN? TURN TO PAGE **5**

You reach the sled with seconds to spare. Barry untethers the dogs, who are yapping and howling already. Doctor Finnegan clambers on top of your pile of gear and holds on tight. 'Let's go!'

You yell at the dogs to 'hike!' just as the trapper launches himself at you in a final, furious leap. He falls flat on the snow and skids a few feet as you make your getaway.

The sled rushes over the ice. You try to keep the dogs going in a straight line, because if you turn a corner too hard, Doctor Finnegan will be flung right off.

After ten minutes, you start to breathe easy. You realise you've given the bad guys the slip for now. Barry punches the air and Doctor Finnegan manages a weak cheer. 'You did it,' she says, then starts coughing again.

'You don't sound too good,' you tell her.

'I'm not,' she says. 'Been sick for a few days. Sorry to say this, guys, but I can't stay with you. I'd only slow you down.'

You pull the sled over by a clump of trees so you can make some hot tea. You know what Barry needs to do. 'The doc's real sick,' you tell him as he secures the dogs. 'You need to take her back to Reshranka so she can recover.'

'What about Guy?' he asks reluctantly.

'Well, we know he was headed to the Aurora Institute near Tompakotac,' you say. 'I *could* keep going on my own and look for him.'

Barry puffs out his cheeks. 'I dunno, bud. On your own? Sounds like a bad move to me. It's a heck of a long way to walk. We're back on the main route, so you might be able to hitch a ride, but . . .'

'I know it's risky,' you admit. 'It's just an idea.'

Barry agrees to take the sled back to Reshranka with the doctor on board, but thinks you should come too. You can always pick up the search for Guy later.

You think over what you should do next.

Barry's right that you'd be a lot safer heading back to Reshranka with him. All the food and water you have is on the sled. If you left on your own, you could only bring what you could carry. And if the food ran out, you'd have to hunt or starve.

It's up to you.

To go back to Reshranka with Barry and the doctor, head to page 53.

To press on after Guy on your own, heading for Tompakotac and the Aurora Research Institute, go to page 64.

'I'll go with Scarlett,' you say. 'Guy probably went as far north as he could. The harsher it is, the better he likes it.'

'Up to you,' Barry says. He looks a little hurt. 'Sure you won't change your mind? You'll love dog sledding.'

'I'm sure,' you say. 'Maybe we can do the sled thing together once we've found Guy.'

Scarlett finishes up her drink and claps her hands. 'Let's fly!'

You say goodbye to Barry and head to the airstrip. But when you first get a look at the plane Scarlett has hired, you wonder if she's playing a joke on you. It's tiny! 'Are you sure that thing's big enough to fit both of us?' you ask.

'That's a Cessna 150,' Scarlett says admiringly. 'Great little plane.'

You stow your bags, climb in alongside her, and wonder if you've done the right thing. The sky looks kind of black to the north of here. Oh well, it's too late to turn back now.

Scarlett fires up the engine with a confident smirk. The single propeller begins to spin. Your stomach lurches as the little plane starts to move. Suddenly you're racing down the runway, then you feel like your legs are giving way beneath you as the wheels leave the ground. You steadily climb, heading up and away from the town, out into the huge expanse of Arctic sky.

'Wow,' you breathe.

'Nice view, isn't it?' Scarlett yells over the roar of the engine.

You are amazed at what you see. The tundra rolls along beneath you. Sunlight flashes off frozen lakes and makes ridges of snow gleam like the frosting on a cake. You're flying close enough to the ground to see the animals of the wilderness: herds of moose, skittering hares, even caribou. In the distance, you can see craggy mountains.

They grow larger and larger as your flight continues. The sky's becoming dark, though sunset is still hours away.

You have the uneasy feeling you're flying into a storm. You point the mountains out to Scarlett. 'Is that where we're headed?'

She nods. 'I've got a hunch Guy might be near the –'

She doesn't get to finish her sentence. A powerful gust of wind throws the plane sideways. Your stomach leaps up into your chest for a second. Scarlett wrestles the plane back under control and brushes some loose hair out of her face.

'Whoops,' she tries to joke. 'That could have been nasty.'

You're just starting to calm down when the wind roars again and the plane is wrenched off course. You feel weightless for a second, as if a car had gone over a bump, then you shake around like a pea rattling in a can.

The storm gets worse. The plane is buffeted in the winds. You seriously don't want to be blown any nearer to the mountains than you are now.

Midway through the worst bout of turbulence yet, Scarlett yells, 'I've got a confession to make.'

'We're not going to make it?'

'Got it in one.' The sound of the engine changes as she drops the plane lower. 'I'm having real trouble navigating. I'm going to try to land. But you're not coming.'

'What?' you yell.

'I want you to bail out!' Scarlett yells, wrestling with the controls. 'Use your parachute. Save yourself. I can't risk both our lives!'

You can hardly believe you're hearing this. 'But what about *you*?'

Scarlett lets out a wild laugh. 'This isn't my first rodeo, chum. I've walked away from crash landings before.'

'So you can land?' you say. 'Great, let's land!'

'No dice,' says Scarlett sternly. 'I'd rather risk *my* life than *both* our lives. You've been brave enough for one trip. Go! Jump!'

You are torn. If you parachute out now, you're more likely to make it out alive. However, you're not sure you want to abandon Scarlett. What if she's hurt in the crash?

To jump out, go to page 94.

To stay with Scarlett, go to page 66.

Barry and Doctor Finnegan shake your hand. 'Good luck, bud,' Barry says. 'Take as much food and water as you can carry. You're going to need it.'

You trudge on ahead, determined to tackle whatever might be waiting in the wilderness.

After an hour, with snow falling all around you, you wonder if you made the right choice. Maybe you should turn back. Nobody would blame you, would they?

Then you think of Guy. You can't give up on him now, not when you're sure you know where he is.

Just then, like a sign from heaven, you hear the sound of an engine. A truck appears in the distance and pulls up next to you. The driver's a jolly-looking guy with a huge beard, and sitting next to him is a smiling woman in a headscarf. For one crazy moment, you think maybe Santa and Mrs Claus have stopped to give you a ride.

'We're headin' pretty close to Tompakotac!' she calls. 'Can we give you a lift some of the way?'

'Please!' you answer. You climb up next to her and rest your aching legs.

It turns out the driver's name is Cletus. He and his wife Suzie are going on an ice-fishing trip. 'Been looking forward to this all year,' he says. 'I just hope everything's OK up in Tompakotac.'

Uh-oh. 'Why wouldn't it be?' you ask.

'It's a weird place,' Cletus says. 'I got friends there. Usually they write me every month, but lately – zip. Not a word.'

'Last letter we got told us to "watch out for the crazy guy in the ice-house",' adds Suzie.

Cletus nods. 'Yup, things are weird up in those latitudes.'

After a long drive through the night, during which you catch some sleep, you are dropped off. Finally, you're within sight of your goal.

Head to page 118.

'What are you doing?' Scarlett howls. 'You have to jump, now!'

'I'm staying here with you,' you tell her. Your knuckles are white from holding on to your seat, but you've made up your mind.

Scarlett smacks her forehead. 'Fine. Your funeral!'

From that moment on, she ignores you and concentrates on landing the plane. The icy winds howl and lash around the wings. You keep quiet and do your best not to distract her as she tries to land the plane in gale-force winds.

It's touch-and-go for a while as you are blown back and forth, but to your amazement and relief, she finally manages a spectacular landing at the foot of the mountains.

The plane jolts, bumps and finally judders to a standstill. Scarlett has brought you down on a more or less level plain, right by the rocky slopes that lead up to the mountains. The engine stutters, chokes and cuts off altogether.

'We made it,' she says, sounding numb. 'I guess

someone up there is looking out for us.'

'I'm going to radio for help,' you tell her. The plane is so battered that you're not sure it'll be able to get you back to town, let alone on to Tompakotac.

Scarlett shakes her head. 'Why? Nobody will hear you. I mean, us.'

'It's got to be worth a shot!' You put out a mayday call on the radio, giving the location where the plane went down. You get no reply.

'I did say,' Scarlett sighs. 'Come on. Let's do what we came here to do. Find Guy Dangerous.'

Although the wind is still howling, Scarlett suggests you head up into the mountains in search of Guy. She refuses to explain further, claiming she has a 'strong hunch' he's somewhere up there, among the icy cliffs and treacherous slopes.

If you think Scarlett's hunch is worth following, head to page 71.

If you'd rather pitch your tent and hope that the storm blows over, head to page 92.

Y ou and Barry guide the sled over pressure ridges and around huge fractures in the ice, covering mile after frozen mile. The huskies end the day tired, but content. You're getting used to sleeping in a tent and living off campfire food.

Barry wasn't kidding about Tompakotac being a long way, but you cover the miles one day at a time. You soon get used to the cold, and even start to enjoy it. But you never get used to looking at the beautiful, snow-covered landscape.

By the time you reach the outskirts of Tompakotac, you're feeling pretty good about this expedition. Then the huskies, all at once, start to whine and howl. Suddenly, they slow down and come to a complete halt. Barry tries to urge them on, but they won't budge.

You go to check on the top dog, Captain Jack. 'What's wrong, boy? Are you hurt?'

The dog looks up at you with big blue eyes full of fear, as if he wishes he could tell you what the matter was. Then he lets out a bone-chilling howl.

'They're spooked!' Barry says. 'I ain't never seen anything like it.'

'It's like they're scared of something,' you agree. You look up ahead to the distant buildings of Tompakotac. 'I don't think they like the town.'

Barry sniffs. 'Do you smell something?'

Now he mentions it, you do. A smell like the monkey enclosure at the zoo, but very faint. The dogs have a much sharper sense of smell than you. That must be what's scaring them.

'Hike!' Barry commands. 'Hike!'

The dogs won't move. Brucie, the smallest, tries to turn around and run back the other way.

It's clear you can't take the sled on to Tompakotac. 'We can't tether the dogs here and leave them, either,' Barry says. 'If they're that scared, they could hurt themselves trying to get away.'

'Or whatever they're scared of could come and find them,' you point out.

There's nothing else for it. You'll have to carry on to Tompakotac on your own, while Barry sets up a base camp here and looks after the frightened huskies.

You get a fitful night's sleep and prepare to press onwards the next day. 'Be careful,' Barry warns, shaking your hand. 'And good luck.'

Just as you're setting off, your phone bleeps. To your amazement, Guy Dangerous has sent a crackly voice message. It sounds like he's saying 'Aurora . . . frozen . . . demon monkeys.'

That's . . . weird. Does he mean the Aurora Borealis, the Northern Lights? Barry realises he means the Aurora Research Institute, which he says is just outside Tompakotac, to the north. So Guy *is* near here. Scarlett was right after all! But how did she know?

You shoulder your backpack and start walking.

Head to page 118.

'So, you're feeling bold enough for a spot of mountaineering, eh?' grins Scarlett. 'You're a plucky thing, aren't you?'

You rope yourselves together and set off. Soon you're clambering up rocky hillsides, hacking footholds out of the ice, and banging spikes in to hold the ropes.

The storm calms down while you climb, fortunately. In the bright sunshine, the mountains look like something from a picture postcard. You'll remember this view for the rest of your life.

From time to time, Scarlett checks a gadget before tucking it away again. It seems her confidence in Guy's whereabouts is based on more than a 'hunch'. You're also sure you see strange shapes following you, half-visible against the endless white snow.

'Can you see those?' you ask nervously, pointing them out.

'You're just imagining things,' Scarlett says lightly.

You make good progress, despite some hair-raising near misses that almost plunge you down the mountain in a shower of ice fragments. Soon you reach a sheltered ledge.

'This looks like a perfect place to pitch the tent,' Scarlett says. 'I don't know about you, but I'm about ready for a rest.'

You rig the tent and climb inside, glad to be out of the cold. After a meal – dried packet soup and noodles cooked with melted snow – Scarlett wriggles into her sleeping bag. 'You'd better not snore,' she says sleepily. 'If you snore, I'll kick you off the cliff . . .' Next moment, she's asleep.

You clamber into your own sleeping bag. You're dead tired, but for some reason it takes you a while to get to sleep. Is it the whining sound of the wind, which never quite goes away, or the soft sounds of mysterious creatures moving about outside?

Hours later, you wake up. The bright light through the tent fabric tells you it's morning.

Scarlett's sleeping bag has gone. So has all of her stuff. So has Scarlett!

You unzip the tent a little, but you can't see any sign of her outside. You pause for a moment. You don't want to abandon the tent and all your supplies, but if you leave now you might be able to catch up with her — wherever she's gone.

To rush out in search of Scarlett,
go to page 75.

To take your time and pack the tent up before
moving on, go to page 79.

It was a trap! Someone had rigged the fuel storehouse to explode. They were probably trying to catch whatever it was that attacked the town. And explode it does – quite spectacularly, in fact.

You get a fantastic view of the town from several hundred feet up. Everything looks so tiny from up here! Then, of course, it all comes rushing up towards you . . .

RUN AGAIN? TURN TO PAGE **5**

You rush out into the bright light of morning. Your boots crunch on the snow. 'Scarlett?' you yell. 'Where are you?'

There's no answer. She must have abandoned you while you were still asleep. That is *so* not cool. You notice fresh tracks heading up the mountainside path. Maybe, if you run, you can catch up with her.

You sprint like crazy, following the trail of Scarlett's footprints. The cold air hurts your chest, but you feel good, fresh and alive.

Up ahead, the path narrows. You think you see white shapes moving on the slope of the mountain, but they could just be blown snow.

Then you see a figure standing on the edge, looking down. It's Scarlett! 'Hey!' you shout to her. 'What's up with you running off like that?'

She looks up at you, her face full of shock. 'You weren't supposed to follow me!' she shouts. 'What's *with* you? You don't jump out of the plane, you don't let me escape . . . you've screwed it all up!'

You have no idea what you're supposed to have

'screwed up'. You're about to ask, when a strange soft *thump* comes from up ahead. You look over and see a sight straight out of your nightmares.

A *thing* has just dropped down on to the path. It looks like a monkey, but it's over seven feet tall, with snow-white fur and – weirdest of all – a head like a black, bare skull. It's *demonic*.

It starts moving towards you slowly. Scarlett sees it coming and says, 'Oh, that's all we need!'

You try to drag her away, but she's rooted to the spot. 'What *is* that thing?' you ask.

'It's from the temple,' Scarlett stammers.

'What temple?'

Scarlett takes a deep breath. 'Listen. Right now I've got nothing to lose, so I'm going to tell you everything and I'm going to do it really fast, so please don't ask questions or interrupt. I've known where Guy was all along. He found an ice temple, and we're right on top of it now. It's a few hundred feet straight down. I brought the plane down in the mountains so I could head straight for Guy. Got all that?'

You gulp, nodding. 'Got it.'

The demon monkey is closing in. It looks hungry. Any second now it'll be able to grab you.

You need to make a split-second decision. You can run back the way you came, towards the tent and away from the demon monkey. Or you could try sliding down the steep mountainside and hope you reach the ice temple that Scarlett told you about.

To run back the way you came, go to page 81.

To try sliding down the mountain, run to page 84.

This town looks like it was abandoned in a hurry. Meals have been left half-eaten. Cups of tea have been left half-drunk. You look into some of the houses and see toppled-over chairs, books people were in the middle of reading, abandoned toys — even a half-finished puzzle on a kitchen table.

You're getting seriously creeped out now. What could have done this?

There's a large building at the end of the row. Maybe that's the town hall; it could be worth having a look at. Or you could check the snow and look for tracks — the people who lived here must have gone somewhere, right?

To look for clues in the snow outside the buildings, turn to page 131.

To check out the big building at the end, turn to page 107.

By the time you've packed everything up, there's no sign of Scarlett. You do make out some faint tracks in the snow, though. You follow them along the mountain until you reach a sheer, slippery drop. The tracks lead to the edge of the cliff and disappear altogether. Did Scarlett fall? Did a giant eagle pluck her up? It doesn't make sense!

Next moment, roars echo from all around. There are hideous creatures slithering down the mountain towards you. They look like huge monkeys with black skulls for heads! You're terrified – and what's worse, you're trapped.

At least you packed the climbing gear. You hold your ice axe out as the demon monkeys come charging in. You could stand and fight them, or try to slide down the slope to escape. To be honest, that looks just as dangerous!

To fight the demon monkeys, turn to page 8.

To take the slope, go to page 87.

Y ou pitch your tent, eat a scant meal and try to get some sleep. Even though you're exhausted, it takes a while for you to fall asleep, because of the constant sound of the wind and the cold hard ground beneath you.

You've been asleep for about an hour when a loud grunting noise wakes you up. You sit up, peep through the tent flaps and see a hulking white shape moving about outside. It's a polar bear, and it's coming your way!

It stops, sniffs the air and keeps coming. To your horror, you realise it can smell your food. It can probably smell you, too! It looks like it's going to keep coming until it's right inside your tent.

Do you stand your ground and face the oncoming polar bear? Turn to page 83.

Or do you rush out of the tent and run for your life? Turn to page 47.

'RUN!' you yell, tugging Scarlett's arm again. This time, she moves and you run for your lives. Behind you, the demon monkey roars and howls, scrambling along the icy paths and getting closer all the time.

You reach the spot where you camped the night before. 'Down this way,' Scarlett gasps. 'There's a crevice in the ice —'

'— too narrow for it to follow us!' you finish. 'Good call!'

You quickly find the notch in the mountainside and cram yourselves inside. It's cramped, but you have bigger things to worry about than your personal space. The demon monkey is outside. Its huge claws scrabble and scrape at the opening, but it can't reach you.

Demon monkeys don't like it when they can't catch someone they're chasing. They get mad. REAL mad. It howls and roars and jumps up and down, and then thumps on its chest. It makes a lot of loud noise.

You remember Guy Dangerous used to warn

people not to make loud noises on snowy mountain-sides. Now you recall why. All the roaring disturbs the snow on the upper slopes and starts an avalanche!

The demon monkey is swept away by a huge rush of snow. That's the good news. The bad news is that the snow completely covers the entrance to the crevice.

Fortunately, you're not buried too deeply and manage to dig your way out. Even luckier, a Mountain Rescue team finds you before you freeze to death. They don't believe a word of your raving about demon monkeys . . .

So you set out to rescue Guy, but it's *you* and Scarlett who've had to be rescued. Adios!

RUN AGAIN? TURN TO PAGE **5**

The bear blunders into your tent. Its huge head swings around, knocking over your lamp and your drinking flask. You've never been this close to a polar bear before without a sheet of thick glass between you and it.

You try to remember what the Guy Dangerous Young Explorers wiki says about bear attacks. Are you supposed to fall to the ground and play dead, or square up to it? You're terrified, but you have to do something – you can't just freeze!

To play dead, roll over to page 116.

To grab your ice pick and fight the bear off, charge to page 121.

Your bravery pays off! You manage a skid down the mountain. You fall and land on a rocky ledge, right by the gaping entrance to the ice temple.

Scarlett isn't so lucky. She skids down the slope alongside you, but can't slow down in time. She lands hard and lets out a yell of pain.

'Are you OK?' you say, running over to her.

She clutches her ankle. Her face screws up with pain. 'It's twisted, I think. Ow!'

The gateway to the ice temple is right behind her, a looming arch of solid, carved ice. Guy's inside. You can feel it deep down in your bones. Then Scarlett clutches at your arm.

'Don't go in there,' she pleads. 'You need to stay with me. We can radio a rescue team for help.'

'But what about Guy?' you protest.

'Never mind Guy, what about me? You're not going to leave me on my own out here, are you? With that demon monkey about? I can't fight it off with a twisted ankle!'

'So hide in the temple,' you shrug.

She lets out a hollow laugh. 'That's where demon monkeys *come* from.'

You really wish you could trust Scarlett to tell the truth, but after she abandoned you like that . . . You don't know what to believe. You take another step towards the gateway.

'Don't go!' she yells. 'You'll never survive the ice temple on your own. If you get into trouble, who's going to save you? Please, I need you to stay!'

You think she could be lying – Scarlett can take care of herself, you've seen proof of that. Maybe she just doesn't want you to find whatever it is Guy's found before *she* can get her hands on it! On the other hand, those demon monkeys are scary, and the ice temple is bound to be dangerous, just like she says. It's your call.

To stay and defend Scarlett, head to page 117.

To take a deep breath and head into the ice temple, make for page 140.

One hand just isn't enough to hold the weight. Scarlett drops, screaming, out of sight. You never see her fate, but you don't imagine it's very pleasant.

Then you hear a rumble.

You glance up to see a white wall of snow crashing down on you. Scarlett's screaming must have triggered an avalanche! You only have a few seconds to regret your actions before you are turned into a delicious human-flavoured ice-cream.

RUN AGAIN? TURN TO PAGE 5

You slide down the slope and almost miss the ledge, but fortunately you dig your ice axe in just in time.

Up ahead is the opening to what looks like an ice temple of some kind. It's majestic – an archway carved from solid ice, probably hundreds of years old, if not thousands. Your excitement grows as you step forwards for a closer look.

Unfortunately, it's entirely caved in, and you can smell something like fireworks. *Dynamite*. Someone must have been here recently, and caused the cave-in on purpose. You get the feeling they were there only hours before. It must have been Scarlett. Who else was out here along with you? You morosely wonder what amazing sights might be in there, forever lost to you now.

Wait, what's this? A box of provisions has been left behind for you, with a note from Scarlett. So it was her!

NO HARD FEELINGS?
FROM SCARLETT X

Well, isn't that just *lovely* of her . . .

If only you'd been able to find out more of Scarlett's secrets. You could have seen inside the temple, and maybe even found Guy. But for now, there are only riddles without answers.

RUN AGAIN? TURN TO PAGE 5

The ice-house isn't an igloo. It's an actual house, with its walls and roof made from clear, polished-looking ice. You stare at it, shrug and approach closer.

A man emerges from inside. He has a pointy nose and an equally pointy chin, on which grows a faded blond beard that is especially pointy. He grins and waves. 'Hello! Welcome! Do come in!'

'Erm, hi,' you respond. 'Thanks.'

Instead of shaking your hand, the man bows. 'I am Francisco Montoya. I bid you welcome to my home.' He's polite and seems friendly, but his eyes gleam with what might be madness. You decide to be very careful around him. 'Would you care for some . . . tea?'

Francisco sits you down on an uncomfortable ice sofa. 'I do not receive many visitors here,' he admits.

'Can't imagine why that is,' you mutter.

'I came to this haunted place to search for the secret of eternal life,' he explains, as if that's a normal thing to be talking about. 'I have hunted for that secret in many lands . . . the fountain of youth, the lost city, the caverns of Xanadu . . . and now I believe I have found it.'

'Seems like a weird place to hide the secret of life,' you tell him.

'Yes!' Montoya laughs. 'This is a weird place, *mi amigo*. Time itself does not behave as it should. The scientists at Tompakotac have their Aurora Research Institute, but I prefer the old ways. Alchemy. *Magic*.'

Part of you wants to run for your life and never look back. This guy is a fruitcake. But another part of you kind of wants to hear the rest. 'Go on,' you say.

'I believe the energy of eternal life is connected to one of the wonders of nature, the Northern Lights. What I need most is someone to help with my experiments . . . someone young like yourself. Come! See the laboratory.'

Montoya excitedly shows you around his lab of alchemical equipment. It's full of flasks, bottles and strange twisty glass tubes. He has to work in these cold conditions, he explains, because it helps keep his body preserved. 'Like meat in a freezer, yes?'

You're not sure if this is amazing or creepy, or both. 'So, what do you want *me* to do?' you ask.

Montoya gets to the point. He wants you to take a specially prepared flask up to the top of the mountains and bathe it in the radiance of the Northern Lights. This, he says, will create the Elixir of Life!

Wow. Creating the Elixir of Life could be amazingly cool! But then again, Francisco seems like a bit of a dingbat, and Guy is still in need of rescue. You feel torn.

To put the rescue mission on ice and help Francisco, go to page 119.

Or to make your excuses and leave, heading on for Tompakotac, head to page 122.

You pitch your tent to wait out the storm. You and Scarlett huddle inside. 'Well, this is jolly,' she says, looking miserable. 'Just like being back in the Girl Guides.'

You feel like you are at the end of the Earth. 'We must be miles from anywhere!'

'Actually, we're not that far from Tompakotac. They have a radio mast. Why don't you check and see if you have any new messages?'

You take a look at your phone. There's one new message, but it's incomplete and you can't tell who it's from. Maybe the storm is interfering with the signal. All it says is:

THEY ARE COMING.

You decide not to mention it to Scarlett.

Then an idea strikes you. 'If there's a radio mast, that means someone probably *did* get the SOS I sent out!'

Scarlett looks thoughtful, as if she was pondering something. *What's to ponder?* you think to yourself. She does *want* to be rescued, doesn't she . . . ?

'We'll just have to wait and see, won't we?' she says.

You huddle inside the tent for hour after freezing hour.

Scarlett seems more miserable than ever. 'I want tea,' she grumbles. 'Why didn't I pack any tea?'

Then from outside the tent comes a strange, beast-like sound, halfway between a howl and a screech. You and Scarlett exchange a frightened glance.

To go out and investigate, go to page 96.

To stay inside the tent and make a lot of noise in the hope of scaring the whatever-it-is away, go to page 100.

You pull the parachute on and grab your backpack. You take a deep breath and get ready to dive from the plane.

'Good luck!' Scarlett shouts without looking over.

'You too!' you say. 'See you soon!'

You hope you're right about that, but Scarlett's chances don't look good.

You fling yourself out. Icy wind whistles up past you, numbing your nose and making your eyes run. For a panicked moment you think you might black out, but you keep it together. As the plane vanishes into the storm clouds, you pop your chute.

The jolt shakes your bones, but at least the chute opens. You drift down and down, towards the open tundra. There's very little to see down there, just ice, snow, a few trees and some scrub. *I'm going to survive,* you think to yourself firmly. *Just like Guy would.*

Thump! You land, roll and lie still as fabric rumples around you. Made it! You bundle the parachute back up, hang it in a tree – it'll only weigh you down – and take stock of things.

You have a lightweight tent in the backpack, along with some food and water, fire-making equipment, a thermal blanket, sleeping bag, and a small pick axe for cutting through the ice. After you get your bearings, you head out northwards.

You soon see the outline of what looks like a town in the distance. That must be Tompakotac!

Trek to page 118.

The tent is surrounded by white-furred creatures like monkeys with jet-black skulls for heads. Your flashlight illuminates their grotesque faces as they slowly creep towards you through the falling snow. What *are* these demonic things? Abominable snowmen? *Yetis?* Whatever they are, they're terrifying to look at.

You gulp, and try to get a grip. Despite their fearsome appearance, you suppose they could be intelligent, or just looking for shelter from the storm.

Do you try to talk to them in soothing tones? Gently turn to page 101.

Or do you yell for Scarlett and get the heck out of there? Scramble to page 99.

Y ou drink the whole flask. It tastes tingly, like ice-cold lemonade.

Next second, you realise your mistake. The problem with drinking an entire flask of the Elixir of Life is that you were already pretty young. The power of the Elixir makes you even younger.

When Montoya hears a baby crying on the mountainside, he guesses what's happened and rushes out to find you . . . and aren't you cute, all of six months old? Well, Montoya never does find the secret of eternal youth, but he does raise you as his own child, and ends up a better man because of it.

Not the most exciting of endings, maybe, but certainly the cuddliest!

RUN AGAIN? TURN TO PAGE **5**

'Right!' Scarlett yells. 'If you won't go out of this blasted tent and confront those things, then I will. Out of the way!'

She barges past you and out of the tent. You hear her scream, and then a noise that sounds a lot like a young woman running away very fast.

Next moment, the tent is torn away from around you. Dozens of skull-headed, white-furred demon monkeys pile in. You don't have time to feel surprised about just how random this is (Arctic Snow Monkeys? I mean, really!) before they pounce.

The result is really not very nice, so perhaps we should show you a picture of a really cute kitten instead of telling you about it. When you're done looking at the kitten, go back to the start and have another go.

RUN AGAIN? TURN TO PAGE 5

You and Scarlett flee into the foothills while the demon monkeys tear your tent to bits. Fortunately, they pause to eat your food, so you've got a bit of a head start, and you have your climbing gear with you.

'Which way?' Scarlett gasps.

You *could* head up a sheer ice cliff. Demon monkeys can't climb ice, right? Or you could head for a mountainside trail, which looks safer and quicker – though the demon monkeys might be able to climb it too.

To go up the ice cliff, turn to page 102.

To take the mountainside trail, head up to page 103.

You and Scarlett make as much noise as you can, banging camping gear together and yelling until your voices are hoarse, but the racket from outside just gets louder and louder. You realise there must be several creatures making the noises, not just one.

'Maybe we should get ready for a fight,' Scarlett warns you.

Do you go out to confront the beasts, whatever they are? Head outside on page 96.

Or do you brace yourself inside the tent, ice axe in hand? Turn to page 98.

'I'm going to try to talk to them,' you say, standing up.

'You're crazy!' Scarlett wails.

'Maybe. But I've got to try.'

You hold up your hands, to show you mean no harm, and walk towards the demon monkeys. 'Hello,' you say. 'We have come here in peace!'

They look at you. Then they look at each other, shrug, and charge at you across the snow.

We want to give you a gold star for trying to communicate with the demon monkeys. It was a really noble thing to do. If people only talked more, the world would be a much nicer place.

Unfortunately, the demon monkeys aren't keen on talking. They only want to eat you. At least you make a tasty snack!

RUN AGAIN? TURN TO PAGE **5**

'Let's climb the ice cliff,' you tell Scarlett. 'I don't think monkeys can climb ice. Even these ones.'

Scarlett hurriedly breaks out her climbing gear. You strap yourselves into harnesses and rope yourselves together. You both have a hammer and a bag of little spikes you can pound into the ice for handholds and footholds.

'Do you want to lead the climb,' Scarlett asks, 'or shall I?'

The demon monkeys are scrambling towards you. You don't have long to decide!

If you want to lead, go to page 106.

To let Scarlett lead, go to page 14.

You and Scarlett cling to the side of the mountain as you edge along a ridge barely wide enough to stand on. You cross your fingers and hope the wind doesn't pick up. One good blast would send you flying from the ridge and out into empty space. It's a long way down!

There's an opening in the mountainside coming up where you could shelter, if you could reach it. It looks manmade, like an archway carved from ice.

'The ice temple!' Scarlett gasps. 'We need to try to reach it. Keep going!'

That doesn't sound safe. You're not sure the ridge will bear your weight. But Scarlett's demanding you keep going.

You inch forwards towards the ice temple, a little at a time.

Unfortunately, there's only so far you can go down an ever-narrowing ledge. Thunder booms, the wind whips your face, and the ice suddenly gives way beneath you.

Scarlett tries to grab you, but she's not fast enough.

You plummet down and down, towards ground that looks like a big, billowy white pillow. If only it felt like one, too ...

What secrets lurk within the ice temple? And how did Scarlett know about it? You'll never find out – not on this run, anyway.

RUN AGAIN? TURN TO PAGE **5**

Nothing moves in the silent dormitory. You see scattered books, magazines and occasional action figures. Nothing wrong with that. Scientists are often a bit nerdy.

All the beds are empty – except one. At the end, there's a hump covered by a blanket. You freeze.

The person under the blanket could be in need of assistance. Just imagine what a scientist could tell you about this place! Surely they'd help you to find Guy Dangerous. You take a step forwards, thinking you'll pull the blanket off and wake them up.

Then you have second thoughts. It doesn't make a sense for *one* scientist to be here, just having a little nap, when all the others seem to have left.

You see the blanket twitch. Whoever's under there is breathing.

To pull the blanket off, go to page 141.

To get out of there and investigate the lab instead, run to page 135.

To check out the canteen, turn to page 44.

Y ou haul yourself up the ice cliff. Scarlett hisses at you to hurry up, but you take the time you need, making sure each step is secure before you put your weight on it. The demon monkeys gather at the foot of the cliff, but although they scratch at the ice with their huge claws, they can't reach you.

'I think . . . we made . . . the right decision!' gasps Scarlett.

You grin and keep climbing. You make good progress at first, but then you look up and see a gigantic figure looming over you from an upper ledge.

You can't see it clearly, but it could be a demon monkey bigger than any of the others.

Do you freeze in place and wait for it to go away? Move (slowly) to page 108.

Or do you press boldly on, to page 112?

As you get closer to the big building, you notice it's not a town hall. It's some kind of storehouse. By the smell in the air, people keep oil and gasoline in here.

Someone has scrawled a message on the outside:

WARNING! KEEP OUT!

That's not very welcoming, is it? Maybe the message wasn't meant for you, or anyone else from out of town. Maybe it was meant for whatever came after these folks, and scared them away from their own homes. Either way, it might be best if you left it alone and investigated the Research Institute instead.

It's up to you, though. There might be important clues inside.

If you want to ignore the warning and open the door, head to page 74.

To head out of town to the Aurora Research Institute instead, run on to page 128.

You wait, and wait. The shadowy figure is still. Scarlett yells, 'Hurry up!' But you ignore her.

Eventually you realise the figure above you is just an unusual ice formation. Unfortunately, by then the demon monkeys have hatched a plan. They start climbing up one another's shoulders. Soon they've reached high enough to grab the end of your climbing rope. The demon monkeys swarm up and, snickering evilly, tug your metal spikes out one by one.

Oops! It turns out demon monkeys *can* climb ice. They just have to use a bit of teamwork to do it. Now they're pulling you off the cliff. It's a long way down . .

RUN AGAIN? TURN TO PAGE **5**

Every muscle in your body screams with pain as you drag Scarlett back to the sheer ice face.

Despite the demon monkeys clawing her leg, she manages to drive her ice pick in and secure herself. Before long she's climbed back up to reach you again. 'I owe you,' she gasps. 'Thanks.'

'Any time,' you say.

Scarlett's quiet and thoughtful for the rest of the climb. When you reach the top, you find an ice cave and take shelter there. Scarlett bandages her leg and hardly talks at all.

It's getting a bit annoying, actually. 'What's on your mind?' you ask her.

She takes a deep, deep breath before answering. 'You basically saved my life,' she says. 'I owe you for that. So I'm going to tell you the whole truth.'

Over the next ten minutes, Scarlett explains *everything*. As you'd guessed, she knows more about Guy's disappearance than she was admitting to. One of the companies she works for owns the Aurora Research Institute, an Arctic science base near the town of Tompakotac. The base was set up to investigate weird time distortions in the region.

Explorers from the base had located an ice temple, which just happens to be very close to where you are now, and sent images to the company's top staff, including Scarlett. Guy happened to find one of those images, recognised the style of the temple and set out to investigate it, thinking it might contain one of the powerful and mysterious golden idols he's heard of. As founder of the Young Explorers Club, you've read about these idols, but you thought they were only legends.

'Wow,' you say, once she's finished. 'So do you think Guy found the idol?'

'I think he got close,' she says quietly, 'and then something found *him*.'

You shelter for the night in the ice cave. In the morning, the rescue team arrives in a helicopter. You and Scarlett set off a red smoke beacon to let

them know where you are.

Scarlett's injured leg means she'll have to go home, but you don't *have* to go with her. Now you know all about the ice temple and the idol, you could head there and have one last go at rescuing Guy.

If you want to accompany Scarlett back to safety, head to page 117.

To set off for the ice temple to try to save Guy, go directly to page 140.

Down below, Scarlett yells as one of the demon monkeys claws her leg. 'They're working together to climb the ice!' she yells. 'Standing on each other's shoulders. These things are smart!'

You put on a burst of speed and keep climbing. Your bravery pays off. As you pull yourself up the cliff, you get a better look at the 'shadowy form' and see it was nothing but an ice block. It does look an awful lot like a huge demon monkey, though. Could someone have carved it? This is a weird place . . .

Even climbing on top of one another, the demon monkeys can't climb high enough up the cliff to reach you. You're safe, for now. There's a hollow in the mountainside where you can wait out the storm. Scarlett bandages her leg where the monkey clawed it. As you shelter from the winds, another message from Guy comes through on your phone. You sneak a look at it. It just says: *SCARLETT KNOWS.*

The demon monkeys scramble away once the storm clears, perhaps looking for easier prey. Many hours later you hear the steady *whacka-whacka* of an approaching helicopter. You rush out of the rocky hollow and see the welcome sight of a rescue team, setting down their chopper within easy reach of the mountains. They got your mayday signal!

'Looks like our ride,' Scarlett sighs. 'Shame we have to leave so soon.'

Scarlett knows, you think to yourself. *But what does she know?* You set a signal flare going, so the rescue team know exactly where to find you.

Any moment now, you'll be loaded on to the chopper and taken to safety. This is your only chance to grill Scarlett on what Guy might have meant. Perhaps you should demand some answers. But on the other hand, if you push her she might turn nasty – and it seems like she's kept secrets from you on purpose. Would Scarlett really harm you? You wish you could be sure . . .

To confront Scarlett and demand to know the truth, go to page 114.

To keep quiet about it and wait for the rescue team to pick you up, go to page 117.

'Spit it out, Scarlett,' you tell her angrily, showing her the message. 'You know more than you're saying, and it's no good trying to hide it. Where's Guy?'

Scarlett laughs bitterly. 'I may as well tell you, since there's nothing you can do about it. He's holed up in an ice temple. We're almost on top of it,' she adds, gesturing in its direction.

'An ice temple? What the heck is that?'

'A temple carved out of the ice, dummy,' she snaps. 'And no, we don't know who made it. Guy was after an idol he thought was buried down there. I found out about it and came to save his stupid backside.' She glares at her injured leg.

'So there's still a chance to find him!' You pick up your backpack and gear and get ready to move.

Scarlett stares at you. 'You can't be serious. The rescue team's here! We need to leave!'

'*You* need to leave, because your leg's hurt,' you tell her. 'I don't. I can go and rescue Guy on my own.'

Scarlett wobbles to her feet. 'Don't you *dare.*

You wouldn't last five minutes in that place. Together we might have stood a chance, but alone?'

You hesitate. She's got a point.

'I've got to try,' you tell her.

'No, you don't. And Guy wouldn't want you to. What's the sense in getting yourself killed?'

The rescue team will be with you any moment now. You need to make a decision.

To push past Scarlett and set out for the ice temple by yourself, turn to page 140.

To cut your losses and let the rescue team medevac you out of there, go to page 117.

Unfortunately, playing dead only works when a bear is *not* already set on eating you.

We won't go into detail about what the bear does next, but imagine you're a really tasty pie and the bear is, well . . . a bear. Get the picture?

RUN AGAIN? TURN TO PAGE 5

The rescue team has you and Scarlett taken by medevac to a lodge, where you recover and receive medical treatment. They put your ravings about 'demon monkeys' down to delirium caused by exposure.

You never do find Guy, but at least you live to see another day. Your adventures leave their mark, though – if you ever see a snowball again it'll be too soon. And building snowmen is definitely out. From now on, when winter rolls around, you'll be a hot-chocolate, roaring-fire and cosy-slippers kind of a person.

RUN AGAIN? TURN TO PAGE **5**

You set out for the town of Tompakotac. A chilly wind is blowing across the tundra. You're glad you're wearing thick protective clothing and a fur-lined hood. A few birds wheel overhead, but that's all the life you see. This must be one of the most desolate places on earth.

The hours pass. You trudge on and on, and Tompakotac doesn't seem any nearer. You knew it would take a while to get there, but you didn't count on it taking *this* long. It's going to be dark soon.

You're bone-tired. You know what Guy Dangerous would say: *take regular rest stops!* That's the advice he gives all young explorers. You posted it up to the wiki yourself, on the Survival Tips page. But then, Guy wouldn't want to slow down his own rescue mission, would he? You have to choose.

Do you keep going to get to Guy faster?
Head to page 41.

Or do you take his standard advice and stop
and rest for a while? Turn to page 80.

That night, after a long rest and a meal, you get ready to head up into the mountains. Montoya gives you a flask full of melted ice. 'It may look like water,' he says, tapping his nose knowingly, 'but when the energy of the Northern Lights enters it, it will become the Elixir!'

'Right,' you say doubtfully.

The needle on your personal Loony Detector is off the scale right now, but what the heck – this won't take long.

You hike off into the mountains, heading for a good high spot. Above, in the dark sky, the Northern Lights are dancing. They're great shimmering bands of glowing colour, like nothing you've ever seen. Their beauty takes your breath away.

You hold up the flask, just like Montoya asked you to. To your amazement, the liquid in the flask lights up! It shines with rainbow colours, like a mirror of the lights in the sky. You can barely believe it but you've created the Elixir of Life, which restores youth!

Once you get over the shock, you realise you have a crazy important decision to make. You have the secret of life in your hands, but what are you going to do with it?

You could simply give it all to Montoya, like he wanted. Turn to page 127.

Then again, YOU were the one who made it. Why not drink it all yourself? Run to page 97.

Or maybe you don't think the world is ready for eternal youth after all. You could just pour it away and pretend it didn't work. Turn to page 132.

Y ou pull out your ice pick and brandish it at the bear, making yourself as big as possible. You only want to scare it, and it works. The  bear turns tail and runs. You have never been more relieved in your life.

You quickly shift your camp somewhere further away, in case the bear comes back. The food you saved from the bear is looking pretty tempting right now, and you're hungry.

To finish the rest of your food and turn in for the night, turn to page 124.

To hike onwards toward Tompakotac since you're awake anyway, head to page 49.

Y ou don't hear a sound as you walk into the town except for the crunch of your own boots on the snow. No faces appear at the windows. You can't hear any voices talking, not even a radio playing. Tompakotac looks totally deserted. A door stands open, light snow blowing into the house. There's nobody around to close it.

This is creepy! What could have happened here? It's as if everyone just vanished at once.

Did they abandon the town, perhaps? Or did some passing alien spaceship suck them up with its tractor beam?

You shake your head. The empty town is giving you crazy ideas. *Keep it together,* you tell yourself.

In the dim distance beyond the town, you can see a group of high-tech buildings. They look like pods from some futuristic construction kit. That has to be the Aurora Research Institute. Past there, the mountains rise up.

Do you want to explore the abandoned town of Tompakotac, trying doors and looking through

windows? There might be a clue here to Guy's location, and for all you know, the people who lived here might need help too. Although you *are* very keen to get to the Aurora Research Institute . . .

Go to page 78 if you want to stay and explore Tompakotac.

Or go to page 128 if you want to head straight for the Aurora Research Institute instead.

You enjoy the rest of your food and turn in for a good night's rest. Nothing else disturbs you, apart from an angry Atlantic puffin that's flown the wrong way and has a good squawk about it.

The next day, as you're packing up to move on, a Mountain Rescue team drives past you in a large snowmobile. As it slows down, you see a huddled figure inside – Scarlett Fox!

You run up to ask them if she's OK. The team leader nods. 'She's broken her leg and she's suffering from hypothermia, but she'll be fine. We'll take good care of her, don't worry. Oh, and the delirium should pass after a day or so.'

'Delirium?' you ask.

'When we picked her up, she was raving. Something about giant snow monkeys. Made no sense at all . . . Anyway, you should ride back with us. There's another storm on the way.'

You really don't want to be caught in the storm, so you accept their offer.

The rescue team takes you all the way south to

Reshranka. You are eager to get back to the search but you do enjoy hanging out with the locals while Scarlett's on the mend.

By the time she's back on her feet, winter has almost set in. You miss out on the search-and-rescue mission to find Guy, but at least the locals take you ice-fishing, and you win first prize in the snow-sculpting contest!

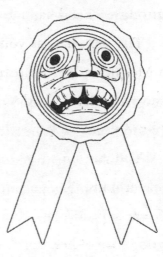

RUN AGAIN? TURN TO PAGE **5**

*W*hoops. You make a hole in the frozen lake, but it turns out the ice is thinner than it looked. There's a terrible cracking noise, then you're suddenly floundering in freezing water.

You try to save yourself with every ounce of strength you have. Sadly, it's not quite enough and you freeze to a solid lump.

Don't worry. When they find you in the summer, you will have defrosted enough for them to identify you and notify your family of your early demise.

RUN AGAIN? TURN TO PAGE **5**

Montoya is delighted. He takes a tiny sip of the Elixir. Wrinkles vanish from his face and his hair turns bright golden-yellow, instead of the faded blond it was before. 'How did you do it? So many times I tried and failed . . .'

A nasty look comes over his face. 'Of course,' he says. 'The trick to making the Elixir is getting *you* to do it. Something about your young age is the key factor.'

'Um, I'm going now,' you tell him.

'I can't let you leave. I need you to make the Elixir for me. Forever!'

You turn to run away, but Montoya is fast and strong, and he catches you. He's immortal now, and you're his prisoner for the rest of your life . . . or until some other youthful dupe comes along.

RUN AGAIN? TURN TO PAGE **5**

The Aurora Research Institute is a collection of pods on struts, sitting at the foot of a snow-covered mountain. It looks completely abandoned. There are aerials and satellite dishes on the roofs. None of them move. You catch sight of strange, paw-like tracks in the snow. You can't tell what sort of creatures made them, but it looks like they were running on two legs.

The hairs on the back of your neck stand up. There seems to be some kind of weird electricity in the air. You feel like you're getting close to the heart of the mystery.

Helpfully, the different pods have signs on them. A long white pod with metal shutters over the windows is the RESEARCH LAB. There's a warning notice under the sign: STAFF ONLY! That must be where all the scientific equipment and computers are kept. You're smart, but most of that stuff is probably way over your head. Then again, it could be worth a look.

A round, fat pod is the CANTEEN. That must be where the scientists went to eat and relax after a hard day's research into . . . whatever the heck they were researching out here. You think a canteen sounds like a safe option to explore. There might even be food.

Then there's the DORMITORY, a curved pod in the shape of a huge U lying flat on the ground. You could get some badly needed rest before moving on.

Investigate the lab on page 135.

Investigate the canteen on page 44.

Investigate the dormitory on page 105.

The slope angles down. You go faster and faster. Just as you are starting to freak out, you suddenly find yourself flying through space.

Whoops. You've shot off the ramp altogether, and into a deep crevasse. It's a ridiculously long way down! You fall and fall . . . wondering if you'll ever reach the bottom, or just go on falling until you reach the centre of the earth. Only one way to find out!

RUN AGAIN? TURN TO PAGE 5

You don't have to search for long before you find deep tracks. As well as the prints of boots and shoes, you find what look like the imprints of huge monkey paws. How is that possible? A shiver goes over you as you wonder just what else is out here with you in this remote place.

Well, whatever was here before, there's nothing here now. The tracks have been lightly covered over with snow, so they're at least a few days old.

Curiosity grips you. Maybe you should follow the prints and see where they lead. The only question is, do you follow them back to where they came from? Or do you follow them onwards to find out where they were going?

To follow the footprints back to where they came from, go to page 32.

To follow the footprints forwards and see where they lead, go to page 137.

You sigh and pour away the precious Elixir, accidentally granting immortality to a passing slug. What a waste.

You go to tell Montoya the bad news. He doesn't take it well. Angrily, he retreats to his lab to work on his alchemical potions some more. You take the opportunity to get the heck out of there.

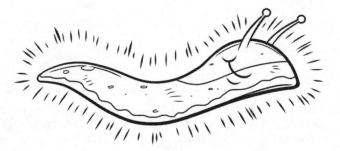

Head to page 122.

You swing the axe as close to Guy as you dare. Chunks of ice go flying across the cavern. You bash and bash again, chipping him out of his icy prison like a sculptor chiselling a statue.

Soon you've cleared away enough ice to pull him out completely. He staggers free, tugging his boots out with a splintering sound, and falls over flat on his face, coughing. 'Kid, I owe you big time,' he says, his teeth chattering. 'You just saved my freaking life!'

'I'm just glad you're OK,' you tell him. 'How did you end up frozen in a wall, anyway?'

You wrap Guy in your thermal blanket and make him a hot drink on your camping stove, while he shivers and tells you what happened. 'It was my own darn fault,' he sighs. 'The moment I saw that idol there, I *had* to take it. I figured I could just rip it out of the ice with my bare hands and run out of here.'

You nod and grin to yourself. That's *so* Guy.

Guy continues: 'The moment I touched the idol, I got sucked into the ice wall, like . . . like . . . like being pushed into freezing Jell-O, you know?'

'Not really,' you admit.

He points at the ice sculptures around the chamber. 'I should have figured that would happen, from all these other poor suckers. They must have tried to get the idol, and it froze them too!'

You stand up and help Guy to his feet. 'Let's go.'

'Wait,' Guy warns. 'I'm not leaving here without that idol.'

You stare. 'Are you crazy?'

'I've got to get it! I can't abandon it now, not after everything! Kid, please, we've got to try!'

It would be kind of unfair to leave the idol behind, since Guy's already had a rough time. But then, it seems like the idol's really to blame for all this mess. You could probably drag Guy out of there with you, if you chose. He's still quite weak.

Turn to page 151 to carry Guy back up the way you came, leaving the idol behind.

Or turn to page 153 to help Guy get the idol out of the wall.

You gently try the door. It isn't locked. It opens silently. You step in, ready for anything.

There's nobody inside the long science pod. Empty chairs sit in front of benches and desks. A map of the area has been stuck up on the wall, with dots and labels all over it. At the end of the room is a whole lot of gadgetry you can't even begin to understand. You think the gizmos are meant to be scanning for something, because some of the parts look like antennas.

You notice one of the computer monitors is still on, lighting up the room with its eerie blue glow. It's offline now, but you can still click through some of the files.

You learn a lot. It looks like the lab was set up to look into weird energy readings in the area. A recent message reveals that one of their expeditions found an ancient ice temple nearby, close to the heart of the weird readings. An ice temple? So that's what's at the heart of all this!

You are amazed to see that Scarlett Fox was sent

an email about the discovery. So she knew all along!

A second email warns Scarlett that Guy Dangerous has somehow gotten wind of the temple and is on his way. He's convinced there's a mysterious and valuable golden idol in there, just like there have been in other temples across the world.

The last email looks like it was sent in a panic by the Aurora Research Institute staff. All it says is: *Demon monkeys everywhere . . . huge ones . . . pouring out of the temple . . . abandoning base!*

The poor person who wrote that must have been crazy from the cold. There's no way there could be monkeys in the Arctic, demon or otherwise! But then you think of the paw prints and shiver.

You know one thing for sure now. Guy must be up at the ice temple. If he's still alive, he'll be counting on your help. You check the map on the wall, note where the temple is, and set out into the snow once again to look for it.

Head to page 140.

The footprints lead away from the village and down towards a small clump of pine trees.

You follow them. You try to think of a tune you could hum to keep the creepy atmosphere at bay, but for some reason your mind's a blank.

The prints get clearer the further you go. There are dozens of human footprints mixed up with the monkey prints. *How can there be monkeys in the Arctic?*

It's as if the human townsfolk were chased down this slope towards the trees by a ravening monkey horde. But that couldn't possibly happen . . .

You reach the edge of the pine grove. Your instincts all tell you to get out of there, but you summon up your courage and you keep walking.

Among the trees, you feel an odd sensation of being watched. Then the monkey creatures start to drop from the branches, one by one, all around you.

The demon monkeys are ugly and white-furred, with black skulls for heads. They rub their paws together and make a nasty cackling sound as they come for you.

In a matter of seconds, you're totally surrounded. You turn to run, thinking you can maybe sprint downhill away from the pines and get to safety. The demon monkeys surge after you.

Now, this is one of those moments where a pair of skis would have come in really useful. You could have zoomed down the hillside like a secret agent from a movie. Just imagine dramatic music playing as you swerve this way and that, sending demon monkeys flying!

Sadly, you're not a secret agent. You don't even have any skis. You make a leathery meal.

RUN AGAIN? TURN TO PAGE 5

You hurtle down the icy ramp. You're going way too fast to stop!

Up ahead, a trapped boulder blocks off part of the chute. You're going to slam right into it unless you do something. Your only choices are to flatten yourself down, in the hope that you can slide under it – or to swerve over to the other side and try to dodge it completely.

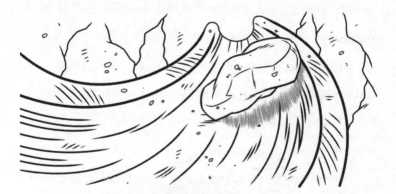

To flatten yourself down, duck to page 144.

To try to dodge it, slide to page 146.

You're finally here, on the threshold of the ice temple. Who knows how many thousands of years this place has been standing here?

You strap on a head-mounted LED light and cautiously step inside, into a huge, vaulted ice cavern. Icicles hang from the ceiling. Across from you, a slippery-looking ramp descends into darkness.

You can also see a smaller opening halfway up the wall; someone has chopped handholds into the ice that lead up to it like a ladder.

To cross over to the ramp, head to page 147.

To climb up to the smaller opening, go to page 142.

Y ou pull back the blanket — and reveal the craziest thing you've ever seen. It's a hideous white-furred demon monkey with a black skull for a face! It lunges for you. You have no chance to get out of the way. Huge claws grab you by the head.

You can probably guess what comes next. Clue: it's not a dance contest. This is just about as sticky as endings get.

RUN AGAIN? TURN TO PAGE **5**

You pull yourself up the ice face, using the chopped-out handholds and footholds. At the top is a little cave that you might have said was cosy, if it hadn't been made of ice.

Someone has made a home here. There's a sleeping bag, a camping stove and some packets of food. Whoever it was, they must have hidden up here to get away from the monkey creatures. There's no way that an animal with huge paws could have climbed up here using those tiny handholds you used.

This must be Guy's camp! Guy himself isn't here, but you're closer than you've ever been to finding him. You look through his things just in case there's anything here you can use. It's what Guy would want you to do, you know that.

You find an envelope. It has *your name* on it. Your hands shake with excitement as you rip it open. You find a note:

FOUND THE IDOL! GO DOWN RAMP, DUCK, LEFT THEN RIGHT. GOOD LUCK! -G.

'Down the ramp, duck, left then right,' you mutter to yourself. You don't know what these strange instructions mean, but you know they're important. You do your best to memorise them before you climb back down and head to the ramp.

Turn to page 139.

You flatten yourself and zoom down the ice ramp faster than a runaway truck. Success! Obstacle avoided!

But up ahead, the chute splits into two. If you panic and don't make a decision, you'll smash into the ice. You need to choose.

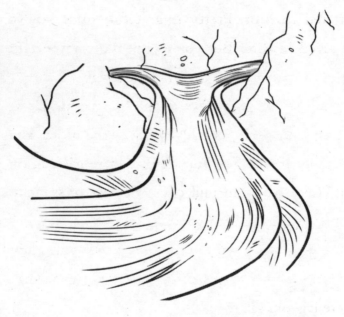

If you lean into the left fork, slip to page 148.

If you lean into the right fork, slide to page 130.

You follow Guy into a long frozen vault. The ceiling at the centre is covered with dangling icicles the size of tree trunks. Their points look as sharp as spears.

Guy doesn't even look back to see if you're OK. He's hugging that idol as if it was the only thing that mattered to him. Pretty ungrateful, since you've just saved his life! But you've got more important things to worry about than hurt feelings.

The demon monkeys come pounding along behind you, their footfalls shaking the floor and knocking the ice free. You think they're gaining on you. Unless you can pull off some sort of stunt to lose them, they'll catch you!

Do you flee down the middle of the vault, right under the pointy icicles, or do you stick to the sides where it looks safer?

To run under the icicles, head to page 156.

To stick to the sides, head to page 150.

You lean over as hard as you can, throwing yourself out of the way.

Unfortunately, you dodge too early and come sliding back down again, right into the path of the boulder. You slam into it with all the grace and style of a duck on a skateboard. Lucky you have a hard head!

RUN AGAIN? TURN TO PAGE 5

You cross the cavern to the slippery-looking ramp. There's no way you can walk down this – it would be like trying to climb down a giant greased spiral. You'll just have to sit down and slide, and hope you don't crash into anything.

You lower yourself down to a sitting position. You wish you had a mat to sit on, but you don't, so you'll just have to get a cold, wet bottom. You let go of the ice and straight away you start to slide.

You pick up speed and soon you're hurtling down the frozen channel like a bobsled!

Head to page 139.

The light shining from your helmet shows another fork in the tunnel coming up. You're going to have to go left or right, because going straight ahead will mash you into the wall, and that would hurt.

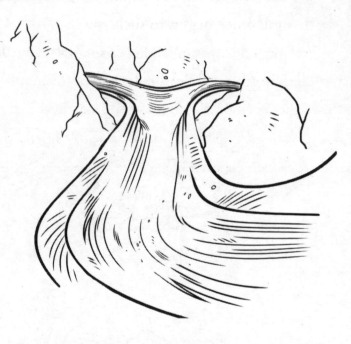

Lean into the left fork on page 130.

Or lean into the right fork on page 37.

Your axe thunks into the ice surrounding the idol and stays there. You try to pull it out, but it won't budge.

Next thing you know, your hands are frozen to the axe handle. With an ominous splintering sound, the wall of ice begins to suck you in.

You end up embedded alongside Guy. Well, at least you'll have lots to talk about!

RUN AGAIN? TURN TO PAGE **5**

The demon monkeys follow you down the hall, and although many of the huge icicles fall loose, none of them land on the hideous creatures. Too bad – by the time you and Guy burst out of the other end of the hall on to the mountainside, the demon monkeys are practically on top of you.

You're both caught, and the demon monkeys have fun rolling you down the sides of the mountain and seeing how big a snowball you make.

You make the biggest snowball, though that's probably cold comfort to you right now.

Cold comfort! Do you see what we did there? No? Oh well, please yourself . . .

RUN AGAIN? TURN TO PAGE 5

You wearily struggle back up the ramp, using your ice axe on the slippery surface.

Guy isn't making it easy. 'We've got to go back and get that idol!' he insists.

'No way!' you tell him.

You look back and see he's starting to stumble off, back towards the ice cavern. You grab him by the arm and haul him up the ramp.

'It's so golden,' he whispers. 'Shiny . . . I want it . . .'

You shake your head and keep on pulling him until he comes with you. Foot by foot, yard by yard, you make your way back out of that frozen place. You stagger through the arch and into the sunshine.

Guy shakes himself and seems to come to his senses. 'Whoa,' he says. 'What happened?'

'You tell me,' you say. 'I thought you were going to go all "my precious" for a moment.'

Guy shudders. 'Yeah. There's something about that idol that almost lures you into wanting to take it. I reckon you're right – it's better to abandon it to the ice.'

With that, the two of you set out on the long road back to civilisation.

'Remind me to make you president for life of the Guy Dangerous Young Explorers Club,' Guy says. 'We'll even get you a medal made up. You've more than earned it.'

Well done! You've rescued Guy Dangerous and kept yourself alive into the bargain. But what would have happened if you'd retrieved the idol, too? Only one way to find out . . . head back to the beginning and try again!

RUN AGAIN? TURN TO PAGE 5

You get your ice axe ready. You can chop the idol out the same way you chopped Guy out. 'No!' Guy yells. 'I've got a better idea.'

Guy explains that hitting the ice will just get you dragged in like he was. He does have some explosive charges. Maybe blasting the idol out will work.

Together you rig the charges, stand back and hit the detonator. One tremendous bang later, the idol is lying in the middle of the room, the ice wall is demolished and the ground is shaking beneath you. You must have destabilised the whole cave system!

Just as you're thinking it can't get any worse, you hear a screech and are met by a terrifying sight. Huge demon monkeys are piling down the ice ramp and into the room! You've already seen a lot on this mission, but this is the scariest thing yet.

To grab the idol and run, go to page 154.

To let Guy grab the idol and follow him out, go to page 145.

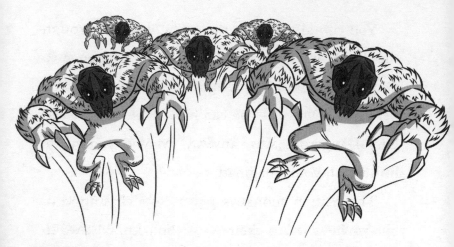

You ou run, and run, and run. You don't look back. The idol channels energy into your muscles.

With the demon monkeys pursuing, you leap across ravines, slide down ice sheets and dodge around dangling icicles. You have the funny feeling you've seen some of this scenery before, and then the feeling goes away.

You clutch the idol tightly and never let go of it. Sometimes you tuck it under one arm when you need the other arm for climbing, but most of the time you just cling to it like a security blanket.

It's yours and you aren't giving it to anyone!

You run all through the night, and all through the day. Sometimes you wonder what happened to Guy Dangerous. He was right behind you, and then he wasn't. Oh well. You can hardly remember who Guy Dangerous was, anyway. Maybe you made him up, in your imagination.

The demon monkeys never stop chasing you, but you're wise to their ways. You know how to jump over rockfalls that they will stumble into, and how to slide down narrow channels that they can't easily handle. So long as you never stop running, they'll never catch you.

So you never stop.

Turn to page 154.

Good call! Although you have to dodge some falling icicles, it's the demon monkeys who have the most trouble. Their heavy footsteps shake the icicles loose, bringing them down on their heads like great gleaming javelins. Was that your plan all along? Clever you, if it was.

'There's a way out!' Guy yells. 'Come on, run for your life!'

With the angry roars of the demon monkeys ringing in your ears, you run towards the light. Next thing you know, you're hurtling down an ice ramp. You *whump* into soft snow at the base, gasping but alive.

Guy holds the idol up like a sportsman who's won a trophy. He looks like he's about to kiss it, but something about its ugly scowl changes his mind.

'We made it,' you say. 'And we got the idol, too!'

Guy grins at you. 'Couldn't have done it without you,' he admits. 'Thanks, kid. You really came through for me.'

On the flight home, you and Guy will have a

lot of stories to share about your time on the ice. You get the feeling your adventures together are just beginning. Who knows where Guy's search for the mysterious golden idols will take him next?

For now, it's time to enjoy some hot chocolate and thaw out. Congratulations!

RUN AGAIN? TURN TO PAGE **5**

GET READY TO RUN FOR YOUR LIFE! AGAIN!

COLLECT ALL THE BOOKS IN THIS ACTION-PACKED SERIES!

Run with Guy Dangerous, Scarlett Fox, Barry Bones and all your favourite Temple Run players.

Your choices will change the story – a different adventure every time!

AND MORE ADVENTURES COMING SOON!